Ling & Ting

Not Exactly the Same!

by Grace Lin

L B

LITTLE, BROWN AND COMPANY

New York   Boston

Special thanks to twins
Rebekah MeiRui and Jennifer MeiDe Reed Kahn
Mae Lan and Sylvie Ling Pryor
Catherine and Margaret Gorman
Alexandra and Charlotte Zieselman
Kendal and Chelsea Tinsley
Mayalin and Kiralee Murphy
Janie and Suzie Romano

Little, Brown and Company

Hachette Book Group
237 Park Avenue, New York, NY 10017
Visit our website at www.lb-kids.com

Little, Brown and Company is a division of Hachette Book Group, Inc.
The Little, Brown name and logo are trademarks of Hachette Book Group, Inc.

First Edition: July 2010

Library of Congress Cataloging-in-Publication Data

Lin, Grace.
  Ling & Ting / by Grace Lin. —1st ed.
    p. cm.
  Summary: Ling and Ting are identical twins that people think are exactly the same, but time and again they prove to be different.
  ISBN 978-0-316-02452-5
  [1. Twins—Fiction. 2. Sisters—Fiction. 3. Individuality—Fiction. 4. Chinese Americans—Fiction.] I. Title.
II. Title: Ling and Ting.
  PZ7.L644Lin 2010
  [E]—dc22

                                          2009028701

                              10 9 8 7 6 5 4 3 2 1

                                          QUAL

                              Printed in China

Table of Contents

Story

1

The Haircuts

Ling and Ting are twins. They have the same brown eyes. They have the same pink cheeks. They have the same happy smiles. People see them and they say, "You two are exactly the same!"

"We are not *exactly* the same," Ling says.

Ting laughs because she is thinking exactly the same thing!

Ling and Ting also have the same black
hair. It grows long at the same time too.
They are going to the barber for a haircut.

"You two are exactly the same!" the
barber says.

"We are not *exactly* the same," Ting says.

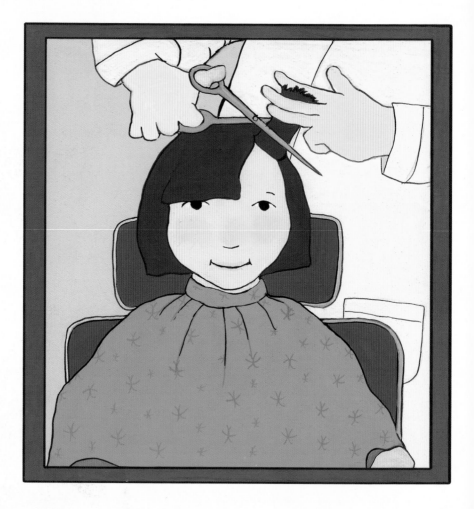

Ling sits in the chair. She does not move.
Ling can always sit still. *Snip! Clip!* The
barber cuts Ling's hair in a smooth line.

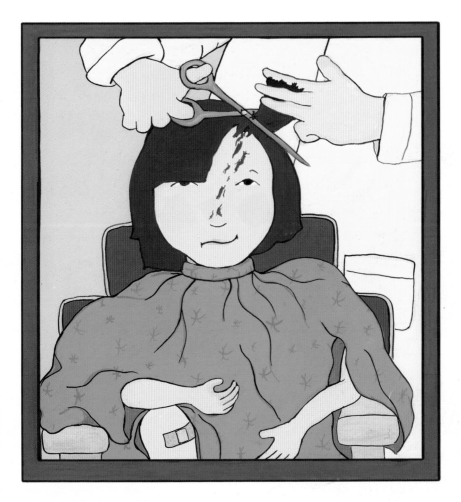

Now it is Ting's turn. She moves her legs
and her fingers. Ting can never sit still.
Snip! Clip! The barber cuts Ting's hair.
It falls on her nose . . .

AHH-CHOOO!

Oh no!

Oops.

Ling and Ting are twins. They are not exactly the same. Now when people see them, they know it too.

Ling is wearing a big black hat. It is a
very big hat. It is too big for Ling.

"Why are you wearing that hat?"
Ting asks.

"It is a magic hat," Ling says. "I am
wearing it because I can do magic."

"You can?" Ting says. "Can you use your
magic to get a smaller hat?"

"No," Ling says. "But I can do a magic card trick."

Ling makes a pile of cards.

"Pick a card, any card," Ling says.

Ting picks a card.

"Now," Ling says, "put it back and mix the cards up."

Ting puts the card back and mixes the cards up.

"Shazaam!" Ling says and she waves her wand.

"Abracadabra! Hocus pocus!"

13

"Is this your card?" Ling asks.

"No," Ting says.

"Is this your card?" Ling asks.

"No," Ting says.

"This one?" asks Ling. "This one?"

"No," says Ting. "No."

"I give up," Ling says. "What is your card?"

Ting turns pink.

"I don't know," she says. "I forgot!"

Story 3

Making Dumplings

Ling and Ting are going to make dumplings.

"People say dumplings look like old Chinese money," Ling says.

"We should make a lot of dumplings," Ting says. "Then we will have a lot of money."

So, Ling rolls and Ting mixes.

"I will close my dumplings tight,"
Ling says. "Then our money will not
get away."

"I will put a lot of meat in my
dumplings," Ting says. "So we will be
very rich."

Soon all the dumplings are done.

"Our dumplings do not look the same,"
Ling says. "My dumplings are smooth.
Your dumplings are fat."

"Yours are dump-Lings," Ting says.
"Mine are dump-*Tings!*"

At dinner, Ling cannot eat.

"Chopsticks are tricky," Ling says.
"They are hard to use."

"Chopsticks are not tricky," Ting says. "They are not hard to use."

"Chopsticks are hard for *me* to use," Ling says. "I cannot eat. My food falls off my chopsticks."

"I know!" Ting says. "We can glue the food to your chopsticks."

"Glue!" Ling says. "That would make the food taste bad!"

"I know!" Ting says. "We can tie the food to your chopsticks."

"Tie?" Ling asks. "That would be messy."

"I know!" Ting says. "I will feed you with *my* chopsticks."

"No!" Ling says. "I do not want to glue my chopsticks. I do not want to tie my chopsticks. I do not want you to feed me with your chopsticks."

"Then how will you eat?" Ting asks.

"I will eat with a fork," Ling says.

"I am going to the library," Ting says.
"I am going to get a fairy tale book."

"Will you get me a book?" Ling asks.
"Get me a book about dogs."

At the library, Ting looks at all the books.
Then, Ting sees a book with fairy tales.

"I must see Ling right away!" Ting says.
She runs back home.

"Ling! Ling!" Ting says. "I remember my card! It was the King of Hearts!"

"That is good," Ling says. "Did you get me a book about dogs?"

Ting turns pink.

"Oops," she says, "I forgot!"

"Tell me a story," Ling says.

"Okay," Ting says. "Once upon a time, there were twin girls. They were named Ling and Ting. People saw them and said, 'You two are exactly the same!'"

"Oh good," Ling says. "I know this story."

"Then, one day, Ling sneezed during her haircut. . . . ," Ting says.

"You mixed that up," Ling says. "You sneezed, not me!"

"When Ling sneezed, her magic hat flew . . . ," Ting says.

"My magic hat flew?" asks Ling.

"It flew to Ting. She put it on and waved her chopstick. She turned the dumplings into money . . . "

"Chopstick? Dumplings?" asks Ling.

" . . . for the King of Hearts. He couldn't decide if he wanted to marry Ling or Ting. . . . "

"Marry?" says Ling. "What?!"

"Oh, Ting," Ling says, "you mixed up the whole story!"

"But the twins told the king to go away. They were not exactly the same," Ting says, "but they always stayed together."

"Well," Ling says, "at least you got the ending right."